BEHIND the SCENES

Saunak Mitra

BLUEROSE PUBLISHERS
India | U.K.

Copyright © Saunak Mitra 2024

All rights reserved by author. No part of this publication may be reproduced, stored in a retrieval system or transmitted in any form or by any means, electronic, mechanical, photocopying, recording or otherwise, without the prior permission of the author. Although every precaution has been taken to verify the accuracy of the information contained herein, the publisher assumes no responsibility for any errors or omissions. No liability is assumed for damages that may result from the use of information contained within.

BlueRose Publishers takes no responsibility for any damages, losses, or liabilities that may arise from the use or misuse of the information, products, or services provided in this publication.

For permissions requests or inquiries regarding this publication, please contact:

BLUEROSE PUBLISHERS
www.BlueRoseONE.com
info@bluerosepublishers.com
+91 8882 898 898
+4407342408967

ISBN: 978-93-5819-714-3

Cover design: Raghunath Sharma (Kedor N Santy)
Translation: Subhas Bagchi
Typesetting: Pooja Sharma

First Edition: January 2024

To
Beloved SUNNY
My "Sun"... My "Shine"

The day is the 20th March 2020. The sun is setting on the horizon of the Arabian Sea. The traffic is stuck on Marine Drive as usual.

Aryan Kapoor, the Bollywood Aryan Kapoor, is getting ready to attend a film award ceremony in the drawing room of his sea facing lavish apartment on the 28th floor of one of the most posh high rise.

Bobby Rawat, younger business partner of Aryan, while looking at his friend asks him, 'Do you really want to attend this award ceremony? It is Film City Magazine's function. These men for the last three years have been just nominating your film, though all know, the award will go to Sahryar.'

Adjusting his tie-knot Aryan replies, 'This year he won't get.'

'How could you be that sure after all? Sahriyar is Moolchandani's blue-eyed boy!'

With a smile on his lips Aryan replies, 'Bobby, Moolchandaniji doesn't like me— does it mean all of his family members dislike?'

Little surprisingly Bobby exclaims, 'Meaning? Oh! Okay; you mean Preeti Moolchandani? Man…. you are just a born….'

Aryan gets him, and says laughingly, ' I know. Anyway, leave it. What to do with our Pappu's film?'

"You mean our Krish's film 'The Surgical War? How much is left of its shoot?"

'I think it should take another 4 to 5 days to get finished. He said something like that. My climax scene with Deepak is left only.'

'Yes; but the situation seems to be a bit dicey. A lot of rumors are flying all over regarding the virus that has spread from China. The authority of my daughter's college has declared an unofficial holiday. Other countries too....'

This virus, the ever tiniest creation of Nature, would within no time catapult Aryan in a situation, perhaps for the first or last time in his life, where this super film star of his time will be pitted against his 'self' and be self-driven to reveal to us the stark reality of life behind the make-belief tinsel-bedecked film world.

Mishraji, Aryan's aged mentor and manager, enters into Aryan's drawingroom and interrupts Bobby to tell them that the shoot must anyhow be finished.

Aryan apprehends something and somewhat inquiringly says to Mishra ji, 'That means, the day's opening collection is not up to the expectation?'

Their conversation roles over the Aryan's recently released film's future. Mishraji, who is very much in Aryan's confidence, tries to calm his son-like star's anxiety by showing him valid reasons for low selling of tickets, pointing to the fact that the film has been released at the end of the month when film-goers' pockets get tight.

Gradually the business will pick up. Aryan's ego gets hurt.

'In the past, never such things were used to be heard', he interrupts.

Getting somewhat irritated, Mishra ji finally tells Bobby, ' Well Bobby, tell me one thing; what's there in this film? Neither any story, nor any....

'Isn't it enough that I am in?' Aryan retorts in the middle indignantly.

Aryan treats the audience as a bloody bunch of jokers. He feels he is here at the top of the ladder because of his discipline, dedication and determination. He has himself made his own destiny. But then, when Bobby asks him, "I will definitely agree with your '3D-walla funda', but....luck? Doesn't that matter?'....silence falls all over.

After a pause, the man of business, experienced Mishra ji, takes over the situation and tells them exactly what is to be done next under the dicey situation looming ahead as per the rumor going around regarding the spread of virus.

As per the plan Mishra ji has chalked out in consultation with the new director regarding 3 to 4 days' shooting schedule, the unit will start for the location the next morning. Aryan, his co-actor Deepak, director Krish and Bobby will take the flight to Chandigarh, and from there take a car to reach the shooting spot in Manali.

Bobby is pragmatic. He advises Mishra ji to be with Aryan, while he would remain there to be with the editor to see that the editing of the shoot portion is finished in the meantime.

Aryan agrees with him and tells Mishra ji to see him at Mumbai Airport.

The next morning on the 21st March, sitting in the back-seat of the luxurious car running on Warli Sea Link towards Mumbai Airport, Bobby tells Aryan, in appreciation of Mishra ji, that he can't believe how he could arrange the whole thing in just a day!

Aryan, having known his mentor well enough for long, asks his friend to look at the booking date of the flight tickets and himself confirms that the flights had been booked three weeks back.

Then, more in gratitude to his mentor-cum-manager than appreciation, Aryan makes things clear to Bobby by telling him, 'He has just been waiting for the box office report of my ongoing film. He always keeps one backup for me. And that's why I still exist after so many ups and downs.

'You mean….

'Yes, Mishra ji knew beforehand this film would flop. That's why he forced me to sign this film 'The Surgical War'. Even he made me fund the film. He knew well that I really need a big time hit here and now desperately, as well as a substantial profit.'

Though Bobby agrees he needs a big hit, he apprehends if it's a huge risk with the observation that the people are not used to seeing him in such a role—out of his genre, with no heroine and bereft of romance.

Aryan thinks, that-very uncanny element may click for him by default, so to say, as in the time of this new govt. in the centre, romance for nationalism sells well.

In between their conversation Bobby's phone rings. It is Aryan's latest heroine Radhika Chauhan's call. Aryan takes the call reluctantly. Radhika sounds amorous; complains with a pinch of sensitivity why he didn't tell her about Manali's outing and finally insists to be with him in Manali.

After a bored and displeased Aryan summarily disposes of her, she lets him know about a negative scoop about him published in 'Film Time'.

Hanging up the phone instantly Aryan inquires Bobby of the said news scoop. Bobby tells him in a friendly note to give it a damn to get focused and assures that the rest will be taken care of by him.

Aryan just blasts at him, 'You will take care of nothing. I told you to see that at this moment no negative news should get out. What the hell could you do? You better ask your office people to immediately Whatsapp me the copy of the article. I know how to teach that editor. And one more thing–you are my business partner; so, stay just at that. Don't ever try to be my mentor, understand?

The car stops at Mumbai Airport.

Bobby tells him to take care of himself and wishes him all the best for the shoot before bidding adieu.

Aryan gets out of the car and joins with Mishra ji, his co star Deepak and Director of the movie Krish. It was a bit late , so, they quickly enters the airport, waving to the cheering crowd.

At around eight in the morning Aryan gets off from the plane at Chandigarh airport. In the exit lounge he as usual faces a small crowd. Avoiding request for selfie he gives a few autographs to some of his cheering fans and hurriedly gets out of the air port through the VIP gate and Mishra ji finds his local contact waiting for them just outside of VIP Gate. While walking towards the van.

Aryan thanks Mishraji silently for his sense of duty and responsibility, and the special care he takes of him. He is moved within by Mishraji's alertness and readiness even in the worst of situations! They get into the luxurious van quickly on the way to Manali.

Aryan was disturbed right since the early morning. As after attending the award ceremony last night, he had to catch the early morning flight, he hadn't sleep at all yesterday. So, as the car started Aryan felt like sleeping. To ensure that he gets a couple of sleeping pills from his knapsack and takes those.

Aryan felt good after having those pills. Because just after the car takes off, Aryan starts drowsing. And within a while goes asleep.

After quite a while suddenly Aryan hears, as if in dream, a distant voice calling him to wake up and see something. Gradually, with the weakening of the numbness of slumber and the call appearing louder, Aryan clearly hears the his co star in this movie Dipak saying, 'Boss, please get up and just look outside. What a scene! Please sir, don't miss it. Wake up buddy… wake up.'

Aryan, at last, wakes up and looks outside. He is simply stunned to see the beauty and magnanimity of nature at its full bloom!

After having a small snacks and tea break, they are presently well inside Mandi. Kullu valley is not far. It's 4.30 in the afternoon.

Aryan's car is speeding through NH-44, with apple orchards donning it's both sides... swaying their heads by the wind from the mountains all around in the background. The last slanting rays of the tired sun is illuminating the ice-capped top of the mountains. The silent song of the nature is being resonated through the billowing sound of the river Bias....Aryan gets flabergastered first, and then he just gets lost!

The eternal beauty of nature with its vastness and enormity overwhelms Aryan.

By the time Aryan crosses Kullu, The Valley of God, he is no more a disturbed, discontented, disoriented person. Thus, when a tired but elated Aryan reaches his hotel in Manali at early night, he wastes no time to go to bed, taking a meager dinner hastily, before that indefinable tranquil spell gets lost. And, this time, without the aid of a tranquilizer, Aryan plunges into deep slumber in no time; not knowing what peril awaits him when he wakes up the next morning.

In the very next morning Aryan gets the news from Mishraji that the P.M has announced total lockdown last evening from 7am to 7pm on the 22nd.of March. In fact, except him, all had known about it last night. Mishraji told him, he didn't want to disturb him last night as he had already taken to bed.

On hearing such disturbing news, Aryan instantly gets stunned and asks, 'Why?' Things get worsened for all concerned when ever-updated Mishraji, gifted with an uncanny feel of premonition, says in reply to Aryan's question, 'As per the news coming out, it appears to be a testing sample like our promo. I am concerned that within two to four days a big lockdown is going to be announced.'

Aryan gets it known from Mishraji that their return-ticket is on 25th night from Chandigarh.

–'That means, we still have three days' voluntarily he utters.

Comes Krish's instant query, 'How sir? We have only two days. Today is already gone. And it is impossible to finish the shoot in two days.'

Aryan rebukes him: 'Krish!! Stop crying like a child. Buddy, location and junior artists are fixed. So, just relax. It's a shoot, not a video game. We shall find out a solution according to the nature of the problem. Rest is ok?'

After Krish confirms that, Aryan asks him for the script and the schedule.

Next, he addresses Deepak telling him that seventy percent of the sequence left to be shot cover two of them; and the rest is with the juniors. He discusses the climax scene with Deepak at length and at the end asks him if he is exact.

After Deepak confirms, Aryan asks his director to listen carefully. He tells him that his estimated three days' shoot will be done as per schedule—but at night; three nights to be exact.

He advises Krish to change all the shots he has planned for day-shooting accordingly. Then he makes him clear about the tit-bits of his climax death sequence with Deepak.

Deepak highly appreciates Aryan's plan, though Krish looks a bit down.

Aryan must have noticed that. He immediately takes care of the situation and tells Krish in a friendly note that it is totally against his nature to poke nose into other's faculties. But, under the given circumstances they don't have much options; and so, he better be practical, not taking things otherwise.

While returning to his room with Deepak, Krish looks frustrated. In fact, he had to swallow the whole thing under stress. This was not unlikely, keeping in mind the long-standing contradiction between a self-made natural artist and an academically trained one from Film Institute—no matter if he or she is a director or actor.

Krish retorts slangfully in extreme bitterness about Aryan to Deepak. He calls him names, seemingly unexpected of a new young director against an experienced established superstar. He, in fact, calls Aryan an absolute dud.

However, Deepak tries to console him sincerely. He sympathizes with his state of mind, agreeing that he is right in his thinking and disposition as well as his self righteousness regarding his forte—a domain, not to be interfered by anyone even if he happens to be an ace star. But at the same time, he candidly tells Krish to get calmed, assuring him of Aryan's acting prowess as well as of his financial involvement with the film; and, the very fact of time-stress under the bizarre situation. Krish remains unconvinced; rejects his offer for a beer-session and getting himself rudely free from Deepak's hand on his shoulder says angrily, 'Disgusting! Just leave me alone. You all are bloody the same.'

In an obvious reaction to such an unexpected humiliating ending of a conversation, failing his best effort to get things reconciled for this debutant director, Deepak just fires at him with words as abusive as possible.

But against all odds and agonies the late evening shoot is done finally, thanks to Aryan's unique performance.

But the deity of luck was thinking otherwise. The omnipresent virus was spreading like hellfire; at least the media thought so; as also the Govt of India. The stage for Aryan's forced solitude was being set fast without his knowledge.

The next day, on the 24th.morning, the Additional District Magistrate and Sub Inspector of Police of Manali reach the shooting party's hotel.

Mr. Dubey, the local DSP , inquires of the receptionist if that's the hotel where Aryan Kapoor has been staying. Getting confirmed he asks the receptionist to tell him that the Additional District Magistrate Mr. Prabhakar Sharan wants to meet him.

Before Aryan arrives, Mishraji, on being informed by the receptionist, ushers the officers into the lobby. Deepak is also there.

After getting settled there Mr. Prabhakar Sharan, the A.D.M, says to Mishraji, 'Sorry to bother you Mishraji. I know you have got prior permission for shooting till the 25th. But have you heard about the latest circular issued by the Central Govt.?'

Mishraji says, 'Sir ji, the thing is that for the last two days we have been shooting at night and resting at day. But I have not heard of any new Govt. circular. What's the matter?'

The rat's smell is in the air, though not intense enough to shatter all the hopes altogether.

Mr. Prabhakar tells Mishraji that he could guess they might not be knowing about it. That's the reason he thought it better to talk to them in person.

Somehow Deepak knew about it. When he makes it clear that the P.M has declared total lockdown in the country from that very day, Mishraji is taken aback.

'Total lockdown means?' Mishraji exclaims!

On this, Mr. Prabhakar also seems to be confused on its implications. But, as per the circular, what he could make out—everybody has to stay in where he/she is and can't get out.

Mishraji is seen somewhat struck by a bolt from the blue! But Mr. Prabhakar assures him of finding some way out.

Finally, everyone gets settled in the lawn with Aryan to discuss the matter.

The very abruptness as well as the interpretations of P.M's latest circular regarding the lockdown all over the country has made the situation bizarre for everyone. All are totally confused regarding its do's and dont's, including the very government officials supposed to ensure its strict observance by the people. As a result, the conversations unfold thus:

Aryan asks the DSP, 'Mr. Dubey, we shared our whole shooting-schedule with you. Now suddenly, in this situation you are telling such things. Couldn't you inform us yesterday also?

'Actually, since this morning a lot of confusion has been going on all over.' admit tingly replies Mr. Dubey.

Next comes A.D.M's turn.

Aryan continues, 'From when does lockdown start?'

Mr. Prabhakar hesitantly replies, 'As Mr. Dubey said, there is a confusion. According to the version of the circular we have received, the lockdown starts from 4pm. But as per other sources, it will commence from 12 o'clock tonight. So I think…..'

Arayan interrupts, 'Let's take advantage of this confusion. You and S.I-sir lend us some extra support. Within 10 o'clock tonight we shall finish our shoot, and by twelve our unit will get out of here. By tomorrow morning they will reach Delhi.'

'What about you?' Prabhakar asks.

Aryan assures him, 'Don't worry about me. Tomorrow evening I've my flight.'

Prabhakar finds himself somewhat in a Catch-22 situation. He okays Aryan's overall plan but gets apprehensive about certain probable issues that might crop up to make things problematic for Aryan to leave for Delhi.

In short he briefs Aryan, though there is no problem in getting his team out of Manali, but, as almost all the local people have already come to know about his shooting spot, it would be better for all if he and his associates remain inside the hotel. Moreover, there are men here who can make a cause out of your shooting during lockdown. If it so happens then it will really be a problem for them to leave for Delhi.

Aryan thinks for a while and inquires if the shoot may be done inside the hotel. Before he is answered, the director poor Krish intervenes, 'But sir....

Aryan instantly waves at him to hush and reiterates the question to the A.D.M, Prabhakar.

Mr. Sharan affirms such a possibility unless the hotel authority objects. At the same time he assures Aryan that the S.I, Mr. Dubey, would stay posted in the hotel to see that no untoward incident of any kind come in their way. He further assures Aryan that he will get a letter issued by the Himachal Tourism for them which they may, if required, show to the check post-personnel on their way while leaving Manali.

Naturally, Aryan heartily appreciates such a gesture of a nice man as he is. On which Mr. Prabhakar, with all humility of a noble government officer says that he has just been doing his duty and, reversely, feels for the unfortunate situation they have been put in. However, he departs for the present with a note of encouragement wishing the actor all the best for the rest of the shooting. Mr. Prabhakar tells Aryan to feel free to contact him any time, though he will try to visit once in the morning to see that things are going uninterrupted.

When Mr. Prabhakar left the hotel, the day– the 25th.of March,2020–was slowly rolling over to late morning. Aryan, with all his intuition and experience, anticipates, if it is to be done at all it has to be done by the end of that very day. At that very moment he knew that tomorrow is not his; or, for that matter, theirs. To him it turned out to be a now-or-never situation. And accordingly he took the reign in his hand for the rest.

Aryan tells Mishraji to talk to the hotel authority about shooting in and around the hotel. As usual, Krish interrupts, and this time instead of imploring asks Aryan what about the continuity, and what is his take about it.

He disposes of the debutant-director by just letting him know that he only wants to finish the shoot.

On this begins an altercation between them:

–'Sir, before you got trapped in a different place ...all of a sudden how could you come to the river side?'

Aryan just blasts at this theoretical naive.

With a bantering tone he chides Krish, "Hey film-school buggar! What do you mean by 'how'? The same way as we got trapped there; twice trapped. The rest of the scene will remain the same. Everywhere in the hills there are rivers. You will just have to take a long shot showing us running by the river, and at the end got stuck here—at the river bed. Then take close-ups. Understand? Any questions? Any doubt? Read something out of textbooks my boss! Otherwise will play test matches only, not 20-20."

Looking at the rest Aryan continues, 'Get ready boys. We have to do it right today.'

Aggrieved and depressed, Krish tells Mishraji that he will leave with the main unit after the shoot.

In the late evening, at the adjacent river side of the hotel, the shoot is done.

It was the climax scene of Krish's film, 'The Surgical War'. The characters, being played by Aryan and Deepak, are supposed to plant a time-bomb at the base camp of the enemy. Thoroughly exhausted and shivering in the extreme cold of the hill in their military uniform they are trudging along the river side.

They fall on the ground breathing heavily while firing is going on from the other side. Aryan asks Deepak to get back to the enemy's base camp to plant the time bomb while he will keep the enemy checked there. But Deepak demurs as he doesn't want to leave his comrade alone. Aryan asserts, telling him not to be emotional, as this is not the time for that.

He orders his friend to move and Deepak departs with tears in his eyes.

Aryan fights to the end. He kills a number of enemy soldiers but finally is sprayed by enemy's bullets. Bleeding profusely he takes out a family picture from his shirt's book pocket, stares at the blood-soaked photograph and sinks gradually....dies with his eyes open.

All crew members get emotional, stunned by Aryan's acting. Krish forgets to shout 'cut'.

Under claps all around, Mishraji looks at his watch. It's ten to ten.

Krish joyfully shouts, 'Pack up.'

While everyone starts hugging one another Aryan chases them to pack up to get out before twelve.

They finally make it and the bus with the team starts in time, leaving Aryan, Deepak and Mishraji behind waving.

All three were happy. They are sort of celebrating 'all is well situation' over a couple of drinks in Aryan's room when he, dog-tired as he was, tells them that he is done and going to sleep.

Mishraji gently kisses Aryan and they leave. Poor Aryan plunges into the bed and soon starts sinking into the depth of slumber not knowing what omen waits for him the next morning. At last the infamous microbe, rather it's being, stealthily creeps into his life for a while to get him off guard.

The star in deep sleep just missed reading the text on his phone: 'Due to Covid-19 pandemic, all domestic flights have been cancelled till further notice.

As luck would have it, by breakfast time the next morning of the 25th March it turned out to be a certainty that Aryan and the other two, by no means, could get out of Manali for an indefinite period.

But Aryan is no commoner after all. So, locally Mr. Prabhakar and Dubey, and there in Mumbai Bobby, Aryan's business partner, start trying their best to find out a life line by whatever means possible to save them, Aryan in particular, from being forced into isolation sine die.

Obviously an ADM of a district could do little in such a critical situation except sympathizing with them and, at the most, lending a helping hand to mitigate, in all possible ways, their local hazards.

But apparently there is a way out, as Aryan felt from Bobby's assurance given over phone that he is trying to find some way out through the concerned minister.

Before he could hardly relax a bit, Deepak, in between conversations going on for sometime on the breakfast table in the lawn of the hotel in presence of Mr. Prabhakar and Mr. Dubey, tells Aryan that the hotel-men have told him to check out immediately.

However, Mr. Dubey assures Aryan, though they are also in a soup for the lack of staff—as the outside employees have already left for their home on the face of lockdown— there won't be any problem for them till tomorrow morning.

But, what after that?

Aryan, to some extent Deepak too, has been hoping against hope like a drowning man catching at a straw dwelling upon a self-assurance that something will be done there in Mumbai by Bobby.

But, sixty-approaching experienced Mr. Prabhakar might have well grasped the implications of the sudden lockdown.

Just after Deepak, with all the uncertainty looming over his face, says 'to whom it may concern' that some way out must surface, Mr. Prabhakar reassuringly tells them not to worry at all about their place of stay. If circumstances necessitates, his house is well there to serve the purpose.

In the meantime, the crowd has gathered outside the lawn. Some of them are shouting Aryan's name, some asking for a selfie with him.

In reaction to his fan's craziness Prabhakar tells Aryan that the security factor is also a reason for him not to stay in the hotel. He also infers, with the extension of the lockdown period the workload of the police will accordingly increase; and in that case, if he gets stuck here there may arise security problems for him.

With this necessary hint Prabhakar takes leave of them not before asking Mr. Dubey to get the crowd dispersed immediately.

Till this moment Aryan hasn't the slightest of hint that the deity of destiny had his own plan to throw him into isolation for another four days wherein he will be seif-driven by a passion he had never experienced, to expose the 'other side' of his starry existence;--the dark side of the moon.

What exactly happens next;—Bobby's best efforts to arrange Moolchandani's copter fails, as permission from the Civil Aviation Deptt couldn't be obtained. And what finally could be had from all the deliberations from Bobby's end, it would take at least five to six days to get the things arranged. So, the only option left to them is to shift to Prabhakar's place, willingly or unwillingly.

Hence, the next morning of the 26th.of March, Aryan with his associates get into Mr. Sharan's big double storied bungalow.

The fact is, Aryan was very reluctant to stay in ADM's house. But he had no option. So, just after Prabhakar got them introduced to his wife(Radhika), daughter(Pihu), caretaker Kishanlal and his adolescent daughter Chhutki, Aryan just asks, 'Anything else?'-- discourteous enough to reflect his irritation.

He is ushered by Kishanlal and Chhutki to his room on the first floor with his luggage. Aryan finds Chhutki coltish and chirpy. In so many words she tells Aryan that she and her didi Pihu had worked overnight in dressing his room. Kishanlal obviously is in discomfort with his talkative girl. He tries to make things easy with the excuse that because this Sharon family treats her as their younger daughter, she takes full advantage of their indulgence.

On inquiry from Aryan the caretaker tells him that the other two rooms on the upper floor are for Pihu's room-cum-studio and her parents.

–'Studio?' Aryan sounds inquisitive looking at Chhutki.

Before she could answer, Aryan's phone buzzes and on reading the Whatsapp message he gets tensed.

Kishanlal and his daughter leave. Aryan shuts the door awkwardly.

Chhutki wastes no time to report to Pihu her first reflection on meeting this ace star. She finds Pihu on a swing in the corridor reading a book. Chhutki hurries to tell her in a low voice, 'Seems to be a bit strange!'

Pihu affectionately chides her, 'It's you who are odd. What is he to you? What was the need for so much babbling? These men prefer privacy. Don't talk much. Now just go and make a coffee for me.'

Chhutki leaves. Pihu looks at Aryan's door for a while and continues reading.

From this moment onwards starts a disturbing phase in the life of a disgruntled and bored self made successful film actor, though to be short lived, wherein he would find his 'self' pitted against him; gradually, getting somewhat compelled to disgorge the venom he had to drink–the very price he paid to find apparent treasure of nectar.

Aryan would release himself through revealing….. but to whom?

Presently, behind the door Pihu was looking at a while ago, in his allotted room a frustrated Aryan lights a cigarette and reads the message from Bobby again. It is a screenshot of an interview of a struggling model, Natasha, who has blamed Aryan for his arrogance and misconduct which she had faced in her first meeting with him. Aryan looks at the picture in the article and zooms in.

He reflects in retrospect:

Natasha is lying on a pool chair in a swimming costume, drinking beer. Aryan, getting out of the pool, takes a shower. Natasha had constantly been looking at him. Aryan throws a look at her just for a moment and leaves the pool unresponsively.

Natasha continues staring at Aryan from another table in the dining hall of the hotel, while he is having his breakfast all alone. Aryan now looks at her with a smile. She smiles back and wastes no time to come to him.

As expected, Natasha starts a conversation.

–'Aryan Kapoor! The heartthrob of girls!'

Aryan blushes and reacts gentlemanly, 'No... nothing like that. I'm an actor. My job is to act and entertain the audience. I just do that.'

–'We are mad just for this style and elegance! I've been a huge fan of yours for ages. I wished to meet you for a long time. Never could think, that wish will be fulfilled here in Mauritius. Otherwise, where is your time to meet with a struggling actor like me?'

–'So, you are an actor?'

–'Till now wandering. Place your hand on my head just for once.'

–'Be self-reliant. You must have a chance, if you have got talent.'

–'Only having talent doesn't work in this industry. Otherwise, what talent Sonali has that by pairing with you in just one film she became a star overnight?'

Aryan smells rat in the thing. He looks at Natasha for a while and stands up to leave wishing her all the best.

Natasha nagging tries to hold him in the conversation and says,

'Hey , stay a bit; at least sign an autograph before leaving.'

–'Sorry, I don't have a pen.' Aryan looks tense.

Natasha takes out a pen from her blouse.

–'Do you have a paper?' Aryan asks.

Natasha comes alarmingly close to him and invitingly says, 'What's the need of a paper, when my heart is out right here for you to write down your name?'

With obvious embarrassment Aryan says he can't do that. Natasa insists.

–'Don't worry, no one is watching. On screen you are so romantic, but off screen...' Natasa still allures him.

Under stress as Aryan is about to give his autograph Natasha tries to kiss him.

Aryan pushes her, says, 'Control yourself.'

Being rejected she shouts, 'What the hell do you think of yourself? You bloody cheap bastard! Maybe a superstar somewhere. How can you do this to me? I won't spare you.'

Some waiters rush to her. Aryan leaves the spot.

The bitter memory of this totally unwarranted incident makes Aryan mighty disturbed. He makes a phone call to Bobby. When Bobby, contrary to telling him something positive, asks him what is to be done now, Aryan desperately bursts out. He summarily asks Bobby anyhow to get him out of that officer's bungalow as early as possible, before he gets bored answering dull queries from family members regarding shootings, drawing selfies with them etc.

As a matter of fact, injudiciously, a frustrated Aryan, in that uncanny isolation, has been demeaning the family of their rescuer in such a crisis.

However, when Bobby certifies Prabhakar and his family as genuinely cultured and also assures him of non interference from any of them Aryan gets a bit consoled.

But poor Aryan's temporary peace of mind gets messed up immediately after, when Bobby tells him about his ex-wife Maria's phone. On knowing that Maria was inquiring about his well-being and she had been told that Aryan was safe, he asked Bobby where she is just now.

Hearing from Bobby that she is in Dubai, disgustingly Aryan comments, 'Hah–and the kids are in Mumbai…well!'

Understandably, Bobby doesn't react to his sarcasm. He plainly tells Aryan, 'They are in Raheja House and both the kids are safe.'

—'Didn't she ask who is with me here?' Aryan asks; his all-pervading bitterness doesn't let him free.

Bobby says, 'Buddy, leave these matters for the present.'

Aryan insistently asks, 'Did she ask or not?'

But didn't get any answer from the other end.

The next morning of 27th.March, the second day of forced stay of Aryan, starts with an apparently more-good-than-bad notion for the disturbed actor.

It's a pleasant morning. Pihu, from a distance, finds Aryan sitting on a sofa in the common balcony of the upper floor adjacent to his room, looking at the beautiful landscape.

Pihu comes to him and asks what he would like to have—tea or coffee.

Aryan unmindfully turns to her with an asking look, says, 'Yes?'

– 'Mom was asking...'

Aryan had heard Pihu's question. He inquires if 'Earl Grey' is there. Pihu doubts if 'Earl Grey' is available in kitchen or not. Aryan tells her not to worry, for it is with him; only a cup of hot water would serve the purpose.

Pihu shouts to Chhutki to fetch hot water in the flask along with a cup of coffee for her.

They enter into conversation casually.

Aryan says, 'So you are a painter. By profession or...'

Pihu replies nonchalantly, 'By passion. Professionally, I am a Psychotherapist. Have a practice in Delhi.'

In between their conversations Chhutki arrives. She puts the tray on the table and smiles at Aryan. This time Aryan also smiles back. Chhutki leaves.

When Pihu makes a move for her room with her coffee Aryan cordially says she may well have her coffee there on the table.

Thus, at this juncture, Aryan unknowingly invites a person into his life, though for too brief a period, to be proved the counterpoint of his persona; to whom he might open out unhesitatingly without any risk.

–'Are you sure?' Pihu reacts apprehensively.

–'Yeah…why?' Aryan sounds a bit surprised.

–'No, actually yesterday we were strictly instructed to see that your privacy is maintained.'

Aryan laughs and gets up to fetch his tea-kit.

When he comes back Pihu asks him, 'Why did you laugh?'

Aryan gives a turn to the conversation and says, 'Prabhakar ji is really a nice person.'

–'We also think so; but a bit more than required.'

Now Aryan starts feeling somehow at ease with this little known lady he is talking to. Perhaps he is getting interested in her.

–'By the way, what type of painting do you do?'

Pihu too, perhaps being rest assured by the body language of the unpredictable star, gets out of her initial uneasiness and says, 'Very difficult to answer. It depends on how much knowledge you as a viewer have of different art forms?'

Aryan surrenders saying, 'Don't have any knowledge whatsoever.'

Pihu cross examines.

–'If someone asks, what type of film do you do– what will be your answer?'

–'Umm…unrealistic.'

–'Hey, why are you saying so? You are such a big star! A film personality of the country! Must have acted in good films?'

–'I doubt; very rarely may be. Do you see Hindi films?' says Aryan with a smile.

–'It's not that. Sometimes I do see.'

–'But not my type of films I suppose.'

–'No, not exactly…I've seen some, but not much.' Pihu does not hide the truth.

Aryan opens him up by and by. Meaningfully he remarks, 'It's good that you see less. And then, what is there in Hindi films?'

Pihu counters knowingly, maybe for Aryan's pleasure, 'I don't think so. Good realistic films are being made.'

Gradually Aryan gets truer to himself. He says, 'Reality less in my films.'

–'A bit less.'

Aryan pauses, and then remarks on something else.

He says, 'I have never seen this combination before!'

–'Of which combination are you talking of?'

–'This…doctor and painter. You tell me one thing–now, if I ask you anything about your profession, would you answer the same way? Because, I don't have any knowledge about psychotherapy.'

–'No for sure. Because, I am very calm and cool as a doctor. Actually, listening to a patient very carefully is an essential part of our job.'

Here, for the first time in their free-flowing conversation Pihu's persona spontaneously gets revealed as the antithesis to that of Aryan's.

But before Aryan could reckon that, if at all, he gets into a bit of trouble suddenly. The moment Pihu finished her take on Aryan's question on her profession, he tells her in a pleading note, 'Look…I took some sleeping pills just to lessen my stress. So, would you mind if I sleep here now for a while? Feeling a bit drowsy.'

Pihu reacts with all seriousness. She closely looks at Aryan and says with a note of alarm in her voice, 'Hey…are you okay? Do you need anything?'

–'No, no…I'm absolutely fine. Thanks.' Aryan reacts a bit embarrassingly.

–'Ok then. I am going to my room. You please take care.'

Before Pihu departs she hears a feeble murmuring, 'Don't mind….

She looks at him for a while with concern and then leaves for her room.

Aryan sinks into deep sleep on the sofa.

But the actor in crisis is not fortunate enough to enjoy his deep slumber. Insult is added to injury in the form of suffering a shocking abominable memory that flashed back in his memory.

In fact Aryan dreamt a stark reality–a bad memory he won't ever be able to forget.

Aryan's ears start tingling with the deafening shout of his estranged wife Maria.

Maria screams, 'You scoundrel! You…you ruined my life.', and throws wine glasses and plates. Aryan shudders in his sleep.

However, he tries to calm her down.

–'Are you getting mad? Have you gone mad?'

–'Listen Arun…sorry Aryan, the Aryan Kapoor! You are the biggest mistake of my life. Going against my papa, my family, I brought you from there to here. Persuaded papa to agree to finance your film. And you…you bastard! You have been sleeping with that bitch! And you know what? Got a perfect choice! Monali Rao…a street girl, a third grade bitch!'

Aryan retorts, 'Maria, mind your language!'

She sarcastically laughs and strikes with verbal venom, 'Mind your language!! Going English! Saale.. couldn't even speak Hindi properly ten years back, bastard! How dare you teach language to the daughter of Mr. Rajan Raheja? Even now, if I wish, I can tell my father to get all your work stopped within seven days.'

–'What about works other than that of your father's? Let it be agreed that I'm a bastard, Monali is a bitch. But who are you? What's your identity except being the only pampered daughter of Rajan Raheja?'

—'Is it not enough? You got entry into the office of the producers, the directors...how? Because, just because you are going to be the husband of Maria Raheja and son in law of Mr. Rajan Raheja.'

Aryan, desperately trying to bring sanity into the altercations, says, 'And that made me a star? Don't have any qualities in me?'

But Maria is too frantic to do away with her tongue of the slum.

With a deliberate banter she screams, 'Of course you had! Brought up in an uneducated rustic family... read in Hindi medium up to twelfth grade. This quality you had. To trap a rich girl like me and use her every way possible—that was your quality! While living with me, you continued debauchery with whores. You're multi-talented Mr. Aryan Kapoor!'

Aryan felt he had have enough.

Surrendering he says, 'You better continue. I just leave. It's simply impossible to ...'

Suddenly their little daughter Ananya comes.

In a sobbing tone she implores, 'Where are you going papa? I can't sleep. I'll sleep with you.'

Maria, with venom in her voice, says to Aryan, 'Tell her where are you going? To which aunty – Monali or Sariya? Why don't you tell her? Feeling awkward before the daughter? But she should know, isn't it?'

Ananya still implores, 'Please papa… don't go. I've to listen story from you. You promised me.'

Maria shouts at her, 'Ananya! Come with me. I'll tell you a new story…story of a selfish beast.'

Maria almost snatches Ananya from Aryan's hold and forcibly takes her to her room. She resists.

Maria rebukes, ' Shut up! Just go calmly and take your bed beside your brother.'

With no respite she drags Ananya into her room and shuts the door from outside.

Maria's tireless stringent attack on Aryan continues.

With note of finality she says, 'Listen, tomorrow I'm going to my Papa's place with Armaan and Ananya. Let me consult with him about our separation. And, never ever think of custody of the children; otherwise I'll just destroy you. You live with your concubines. Now you won't have to call them secretly.'

Aryan tries his best not to be intimated; rather, as less as possible.

He reacts, 'Now you are switching again. What exactly do you mean by that?

–'Oh! You didn't understand anything I told you? How innocent! Didn't you call Taniya Shetty here last Saturday when I went with the children to our Lonavala farmhouse?'

Still Aryan makes effort whatever patience he had been left with to hold himself and sound rational in a matter- of-fact way.

–'So? She came because she had some work. And she left within just half an hour. Mishraji was with her.'

But, so obsessed with doubting-mania Maria has been, she is relentless up to thrashing Aryan to the hilt.

Maria says, 'Don't even utter the name of that bloody tout in front of me. And I don't think you could handle a wild bitch like Tania even for half an hour–little difficult at your age.'

'Mariaaaaa!!!', screams Aryan, and hits hard on a glass-top table.

Wakes up Aryan, sweating. He finds Pihu and Mishra ji standing before him with concern looming over their faces.

Pihu inquires if he is okay and requests him to have a glass of water. She doesn't wait for his nod, passes him a glass of water

Aryan finishes the glass. He finds a shawl on him. He is somewhat awkwardly surprised to see them around him with concern. However, after he is briefed by them about their worry regarding him, Aryan hurriedly claims that he is absolutely fine.

By then it is lunch time. Mishraji a bit hesitantly wants to know if he would like to have his lunch sent to his room.

Aryan says, 'Yes', and just strides towards his room without a further word; enters into and shuts the doors.

Mishraji and Pihu, both get anxious about Aryan in their own ways. Obviously, having been the very mentor of this scratch-to-star-turned actor, his worry about Aryan is far deeper.

Mishraji comes to him at night to call him for dinner, set on the ground floor's dinning hall and finds him having scotch in the balcony. Aryan waves signaling his disinterest.

Mishraji stops. Involuntarily, somewhat triggered by the anxiousness he had in the back of his mind about this idiosyncratic actor, he makes a move to lift Aryan's spirit, if possible.

After the necessary pause he fondly says to Aryan, 'Should I tell you something?'

–'Hmm..', Aryan hums.

–'Not only we, all there below know that you're disturbed. But if you help your good sense a bit, there is no reason for you to remain depressed for so long. It's your right decision at the just moment that got the shooting completed. That too, before time!

The whole footage has reached the editor. From tomorrow post-production works will start in his home studio. The Assistant Director will also be with him.

On the other side, Bobby is also trying hard to get us out of here. Thus, everything is going almost okay. Whatever little hazards left have been well taken care of by these people.

Look, it is well confirmed that we have no way but to stay here for another few days. And then, you've no urgent work in Mumbai. Neither too any one is waiting there for you. Everyone is confined into their own little shelter out of fear. On return, you've to be in 14 days' quarantine. In that situation you won't be able to meet your children also.

So, just take it as a break and enjoy. The place is beautiful. The men are nice. You better give yourself a few days' holiday leaving your tension aside.

Live the present with an open mind and get back to Mumbai fresher. There are so many things for you to do in the coming days.

And I give you guarantee on one thing—this film will run; it's going to be a bumper hit. It's my challenge.

Now you give me words, from tomorrow onwards, for the rest of the period we are here, you will try to be at ease with yourself and others, forgetting your hangover. Don't remain tense unnecessarily. Talk to the people…or, sing! How long you haven't sung! Let alone hum!'

Just then Pihu happens to cross through the balcony and overhears Mishraji's last words.

Instantly she inquires of Mishraji, 'Who sings?' And then, guessing 'who' that might be, asks Aryan, 'You? Really you are a superhero! Dancing, singing, acting….all in one! And you were struck to learn that I know two things only!'

Mishraji inquires whether Pihu had her dinner. Pihu confirms and leaves for her room bidding good night to them. Mishraji too leaves.

Aryan makes another drink. He leans back on the sofa looking at the swing lightly being swayed by the breeze. He sips the whisky and down goes the memory lane……

Ananya's laughter rings in his ears. Aryan enters into his bungalow-lawn. It's early evening.

Ananya is laughing out of pure joy as her brother Armaan pushes the swing she is on higher. Seeing her father coming, instinctively Ananya gets off the swing out of excitement and runs towards Aryan. The swing sways back and hits her head in the back. She instantly falls on the lawn. Aryan rushes and lifts her onto his lap. He looks miserably perturbed and tells his son to phone the doctor.

Dr. Kulkarni comes and on examination finds the thud not that serious. He tells Aryan not to worry at all and advises him just to apply ice pack at the place of the blow from time to time.

On his leaving, Aryan comes near Ananya's bed. Armaan confesses that it's he who is responsible for the mishap. Perhaps he might have thought, he shouldn't have swung it too high.

Aryan lifts the mood of the whole situation– first by calling his little son a champ and then telling him that it was none of his fault. Next, pointing at his elder sister says to Armaan, '...And look at her...how brave she is!' Finally, he kisses Ananya's forehead, making the whole atmosphere bright and happy.

The children get infected with the positivity of the ambiance, thanks to their father. The boy just bubbles, leaving the repentance well behind.

Armaan says to Aryan, 'Dad, Ananya has made something for you.'

Ananya warns, 'Bhaiya....no!'

Aryan inquires, 'Well, what's that?'

Armaan takes out a picture from her school bag. Ananya closes her eyes and hides her face with her palms.

It's a sketch of Aryan making him look like a Batman. Below it is written: 'My dad is a superhero!'

With a smile, brimming with the affection of a father, Aryan comes near Ananya's bed and asks his daughter with his eyes flickering with jocularity, 'So…who is superhero?'

Ananya is all smiles; says, 'Dad.'

Aryan tickles Ananya. She laughs……

Aryan is still boozing. It seems, Mishraji's low-key counseling hasn't worked at all.

Pihu, maybe for a break from reading a book—which is her regular practice before going to sleep—opens her door. And she sees Aryan still sitting on the sofa in the common balcony.

She comes near and asks Aryan, 'Didn't you go to your bed yet?'

Aryan doesn't reply. In fact, he is a bit high.

Pihu doesn't give up. She is different, enough self-assured not to get awed or overwhelmed by the antics of a self-obsessed superstar.

She continues, 'Chhutki was telling she has read in some magazine that you take your bed by nine! Maintain a steady lifestyle.... that's the secret of your success!'

–'Yes...might have said, so?'

Pihu is not to buzz. She instantly reacts, 'But in reality...actually I told Chhutki, people say anything to their fans and followers...

Aryan interrupts, 'Five cores!'

Pihu quips, 'Sorry?'

High he already was; now, being hit in the roof by such nonchalant ask Aryan erupts, 'In social media itself I'm followed by five core fans! Outside that it's unaccountable in a land of 140 cores. They are always on their feet to hear something from me... anything. And if, by chance, I'm pleased to answer someone's quiry live, it turns out to be a red letter day for that poor fellow. Understand? You're a psychotherapist... you should know all this.'

Unwaveringly Pihu keeps on eyeing Aryan with a psychiatrist's look.

He defiantly tells her that she understands nothing. People like her don't understand.

Pihu does not buckle. She plainly asks the tipsy star about what thing he is talking about.

And it starts working. Aryan's inner feelings begin unveiling themselves. Aryan exposes himself to his counterpart unhesitatingly.

Aryan bubbles out, 'This public, you know, is a bitch-thing. Always demanding. Like everyone, like us…never-ending. The whole life is spent in fulfilling their demands. They are to be reared…by giving my own time, by presenting my image. By giving excellent talks. And then one day, suddenly, forgetting everything they start switching to some other one.

–'But, are they not the same men who indulged you the most?' Pihu hits the bull's eye.

Aryan defends himself, says, 'Not without price of course! Ten years of long struggle is behind that. So many impediments… insults… immeasurable sacrifices! After all, it had not been an easy ride. Today morning you told me that you're a psychotherapist. In a way you people are a doctor of mind and heart, isn't it? So, you must be knowing the unseen part of our thoughts?'

Pihu, as a psychotherapist, thought she has had enough to read the mind of this successful self-possessed, egoist but ever-uncertain Bollywood star. So she feels sympathetic, rather considerate about Aryan.

Somewhat consolingly Pihu says, 'Look—it's not like that. Yes, I'm a psychotherapist all right. My job is to nurture patient's psyche troubled with different kinds of feelings and reflections. But then, you are a big-time celebrity of our country and we all are really proud of you. I really, rather honestly don't want to get into it further, because then, many an inner story will come out which, to my understanding of things, would not be proper for your professional career. And most importantly, you are our guest. We all should take care of you as you are tired and tensed. I'm really sorry to bother you at this hour of night. It's midnight. You please take a rest.'

But Aryan impulsively has already got attracted to this person of a kind, he has ever encountered. He is up to talking to her, to tell her the inner truth of his tinsel existence.

No sooner Pihu had finished, Aryan says, 'No-no; you need not be sorry. I want to speak out. I…I just want to talk to you.'

Pihu wonders! She says, 'You want to tell your untold stories and millions of your fans don't listen to that…. it's just incredible!'

Pihu's spoken words now bring Aryan, finally, into confession-mode.

He grimly says, 'Nobody has any interest whatsoever in the very truth of the matter. Everyone wants to hear tailor-made artificial anecdotes of the make-belief world of a superstar. Like this story of going to bed at nine and getting up at five, which is also properly scripted and finely filtered to cater to the demands of the audience. And we too can't say anything out of this script lest our professional interest gets hampered. The products sell, the business runs on our image, on what we utter publicly '

Pihu, unknowingly, provokes Aryan, saying, 'But what's wrong in that? I mean, so long as it is good for everyone?'

Aryan delves into his heart, says, 'But young lady, that's not me! I've a totally different identity also! Everybody's focus is on what I, Aryan

Kapoor the superstar, say! But none ever wants to know about my heart ... .what my heart craves to tell!'

Pihu directly asks, 'So, what does your heart crave to speak out? And that too, to me only?'

Aryan truly tells Pihu, 'After a long-long time, I don't remember when it occurred to me last time, I felt like opening myself to someone. But again, I think…..

Pihu interrupts, 'That it won't be proper to get emotional for a while, lest I post your story in the social media tomorrow. Isn't it?'

Now Aryan has nothing to hide from Pihu as he feels at ease with this odd-man-out person possessing a strikingly different nature and demeanor.

He clearly says, 'Because of my profession and the status I hold therein, I've to deal with every type of person. And, incidentally, sixty percent of them happen to be women. So, I understand them quite well. You are, definitely, not one of them. Moreover, by sharing heart's craving with a mental doctor I may have a chance of having some tips…who knows?'

Inwardly Pihu enjoys the compliment. Gleefully she asks, 'So much confidence in me within twenty four hours! That's interesting!'

Aryan has not been drinking for quite a while; may be by default, as he had already finished his bottle by the time Pihu arrived. Might be he needed no more, as Pihu's unaffected persona and likeable company in some way helped the disturbed man release himself to an extent.

With the clarity of voice of a relieved person Aryan reminds Pihu, may be himself too, 'Hey, I'm sorry. I just forgot the time. It's 12.30! I've held you so long! You must now go to sleep. It will look odd otherwise.'

Aryan's relaxed body language does not escape Pihu's notice. Presently she has got really interested in exploring the star's psyche. In fact, as a psychotherapist as well as a woman, she feels interested in Aryan; more as a man than a case study.

Reassuringly Pihu tells him, 'It's okay. I'm fine. By the way, how did it come into your mind that you were to come into this acting-thing; rather, to be an actor? Because, I had heard that you stepped into this film industry at a very young age.'

Finally, finding Pihu's uninhibited gesture inviting and her interest in him genuine, Aryan let himself loose. Thus began the unveiling of the released soul of a film superstar.

To her question Aryan replied, 'It was Mishraji. I am his find. It was he who made Aryan Kapoor out of Arun Kapoor. In my struggling days Mishraji had been my next door neighbour. My father did a small job in a jute mill. His salary was just enough for our six-member family to survive somehow. So, proper education had to be sacrificed.

I wanted to study beyond twelfth standard, though singing and body- building attracted me more. Mishraji knew that. He was aware of the fact that our family needed more income. One of his distant relatives was in the film industry, connected to some production unit. Relying on him Mishraji came to Mumbai leaving Barely, and became assistant production manager. Then, after my father's demise he called me there. I was just twenty two then. For next four years did production jobs…acted as extra…did even body-double roles. From modeling for small local brands to doing sales job–did everything that came in the way. Along with all this, used to sing in a bar too.

Then one day Mishraji came excited to tell me that there was an audition for me. I gave the audition. They also liked it.

Pihu interrupts excitedly, 'And you became a hero!'

Aryan smiles, then says, 'If only I could! Shooting began. Continued for 15 -16 days. I really worked very hard. Everyone in the set was praising me too. But suddenly a rift among the financiers cropped up and all work got stopped the very next week.'

–'What? Your hard work… everything turned fruitless!' Pihu almost screamed.

Aryan, in a consoling tone, says, 'No, everything didn't turn futile. Once again Mishraji came to my rescue. He somehow got the shooted reels out from the camera department and made a show-reel out of that by the editor.

Then, that show-reel getting passed through various hands somehow reached top producer-director of the time Mr. Balraj Sharma; and I got my first big-banner film. But my role was the second lead. The hero was Balraj sir's favourite and lucky star Sahryar Khan.'

Pihu got really excited and curiously asked, 'Wow! With Sahryar Khan! How was the experience?'

Presently Aryan just says, 'I learnt a lot of things from him—all those things I didn't know before. For the first time I saw what stardom means. As if, he kept all hypnotized; even a senior director like Mr. Balraj Sharma!'

Aryan narrates his first hand experience of meeting Sahryar Khan to Pihu.

I was standing near the studio floor, reading the script. The Assistant Director came there to tell me that Sahryar Sir wanted to meet him.

He took me to Sahryar's vanity van. The big star greeted him gleefully with a friendly gesture telling me that he had already heard a lot of praise about him from none other than Balraj sir himself; and that in fact made him think of meeting me before going into the set.

I was like, obviously, got overwhelmed by such a human gesture. He said that that was really so kind of him.

Sahryar, with a view to apparently make the debutant actor more comfortable and at the same time to really impose his persona beforehand on him in a roundabout way, said to him that it is a kind of his responsibility to make his co-actors feel comfortable for the betterment of the film. Because, he added, it is natural for a new actor to get awed in the presence of a big actor. And Sahryar, as he told then, doesn't want to waste time. He hates retakes.

But as a new but a prepared actor, I told him candidly that he wouldn't have any problem as such and Sahryar too would not have to give retake.

Sahryar exclaimed, and said in a tone of suppressed sarcasm, 'O, really?'

Then he turned towards his secretary and said, 'I told you Shanon. That's why I want to work with these new actors. Look at his confidence! Great! By the way, do you want to have something, drinks, fruits..?'

I thankfully said, 'No sir', adding, he has had his breakfast with his unit-fellows.

He said, 'Okay, let's then meet in the set.'

Sahryar further added reassuringly that because Balraj sir had liked him, Aryan is like his younger brother, and he could call him any time he is in a problem.

Having heard upto this, Pihu commented that in that case Aryan's first meeting with Sahryar must have been a success.

But Aryan, with a bitter smile said that the whole prologue had in fact been an eye wash. The hypocrite presented a totally different face in the set.

Referring to a couple of dialogues between him and Sahryar, Aryan tells Pihu—who at the moment is all ears—that the crooked star allowed him to throw just half of his first dialogue and interrupted with the loud shout of 'cut-cut-cut'. And then, addressing all around including the dumb-faced director, the so-called superstar shouted at the height of his pitch (here Aryan quotes Sahryar),

'Hey Aryan…come here. What are you doing man? Why the hell are you delivering in such low pitch? What are you trying to prove? That you're correct and I'm too loud? I already told you before the shoot that I hate retakes. Balraj sir, what's this? What kind of acting is this?'

Reflecting on that bitter experience Aryan says to Pihu, 'Actually, that very moment Sahryar smelt danger. He felt instantly that my under-acting as well as my style of dialogue-delivery vis-a-vis his repeated mannerism and cliché style of loud acting is a threat to him. That's why, right on the first moment on the very set, he demeaned my style of acting, my technique of voice modulation, the way I throw my dialogue, and even my English pronunciation. And he did that deliberately to thoroughly insult me in front of all. So that, I am proved a laughing stock to them.

At the end, when none of his foul play worked, he pressurized Balraj sir to get all of my important scenes scissor just before the release of that film to make a mockery of my role.

–'Then?' eagerly asks Pihu.

Again my new struggle began. But this time the mode and level of struggle was different. Because, as by that time I had some exposure as another actor to the viewers, I needed to maintain certain status—a necessary requirement of the film world.

That time I needed a standard flat, at least a second hand car and to have Mishraji as my secretary. And to get all this done I had three options. To do side roles with Sahryar and the likes, shift to television, or, go for the regional films. I went for the last option and for the next 3-4 years acted in Kannada, Malayalam, Bengali, even in Bhojpuri films. But always did the lead roles.

Then one day, suddenly the Malayalam director Ratnam Vijay sir asked me if I've any problems acting in Hindi films. He was a senior director. That time he probably forgot that actually I am from the Hindi film industry. In fact, he was to make the Hindi version of a super hit Malayalam film. The producer was pressurizing to take Sahryar for the lead role, but Ratnam sir was adamant for me. The producer had got Sahryar signed for the role, along with the blue-eyed girl Riyanka Tanwar. But he could not convince Ratnam sir.

Ultimately the producer had to agree to Ratnam sir's proposal and I returned back to the Hindi film industry after about four and half years with the biggest block-buster of my film career 'Blind', with Sahryar's favourite heroine Riyanka!'.

Pihu feels happy, says, 'Yaa, it was really one of your best performances.'

Aryan now feels more involved with his ardent and knowledgeable listener.

He emphatically says, 'I had to do it. I knew that Sahryar would leave no stone unturned to stop this film. That's why I poured all my acting-forte and experience into this role, so that he can't say a single negative word about my performance. The film turned out to be a super hit and then started the third chapter of my life.'

–'Do you remember the day you met Sahryar again?'

–'Can anyone forget his first love and first revenge?'

–'So you could not forget that first day's incident?'

–'No, didn't forget. But could have never thought of it again, had the ever-envious Sahryar not reminded me of that one evening.'

Pihu's eagerness is on the rise…..

Aryan, telling the inner stories of his life to someone trusted, feels released in emptying the vessel of his deep wounds he suffered during his struggling days. Deep in his heart he gets reveled with the drunkenness of letting his emotion flow.

Both are absolutely oblivious of the delicacy of the circumstances as well as the criticality of the hour. It is past midnight.

Aryan continues, 'It was a Sunday evening. By that time I had shifted to my new flat at Versova. However, everyone had left after the next film's shooting-script had been narrated. Mishraji too was about to leave when the doorbell rang.

Mishraji opened the door. I saw two men standing with a huge flower bouquet. I walked to the door. One of the two said to me that that was sent by their "Sir".

I took the bouquet. Mishraji left after hurriedly finishing his peg. I shut the door and looked at the bouquet closely and found a card fixed to it. I took the card and opened it. It was sent by none other than Sahryar Khan, wherein he wrote that if I had been so confident why should I have sabotaged the scheme of things; I could have just wanted and he would have given me the role just that way.

I rushed to the window and looked down. There was a black Mercedes parked under the light post.

I knew he was in the car. I wasted no time to dial him. He took my call. I told him that he should have known much before that if at all I had to ask for what, I would have wanted five years back. But then, can the pleasure one has in winning the desired thing from someone, be had by just begging for that? Then I thanked him for the bouquet.

I came successful in irritating the self-possessed man to that extent where one speaks his mind—a jealous man's ever-unhappy mind.

–'What did he say in reply?' Pihu is almost on her toes out of inquisitiveness.

–'He first called me a "bastard"—not unexpected of a person of his mindset. Then, as a frustrated desperate man of such character should say, he told me that so many people like me came and went away; only one lion can stay in a forest;---a damn cliché to say the least.

–'And, your reply?' Pihu asks with the excitement of adolescence.

–'I just let him know that from then onwards, such nonsense would just cease to happen. I told him that it took me five years to figure out how you became a lion in this forest, having made others around you a flock of sheep. I finished by warning Sahryar that there would really be one lion in one forest as he claimed; but unfortunately that wouldn't be him at least. And before hanging up my phone bid him good night.'

Aryan has by this time ejected himself off a lot. He feels emptied to a good extent.

So long, under the narcotic spell of unloading himself through talking to some trusted one, Aryan didn't need a drink. But that feel of intoxication, of speaking one's heart out to an empathetic listener, has almost waned. Now he feels a craving in him for getting that lightness of being drunk back. He feels thirsty.

Aryan says to Pihu, 'Excuse me, I'm just coming.' He rushes to his room and within a minute comes back with a new bottle of scotch, makes a peg, gives a sip and turns towards Pihu.

Pihu was waiting with her remark on Aryan's long delivery. Looking at him intensely she says to him, 'So, you took a fitting revenge for the first day's encounter, isn't it?'

A couple of sips make Aryan at ease with himself.

He feels composed. In a calm voice he says to Pihu, 'Well, it's true that I didn't forget; rather, couldn't be able to forget ever the way he behaved with me on the very first day of our shooting. But I did never manipulate anyone or sabotage anything. This bloody allegation regarding Riyanka that I've somewhat eloped her to partner with me, which he calls sabotage, is nothing but the reaction of his own insecurity-feeling.'

Pihu wants to know more. She delves into Aryan's psyche. She asks, 'So you want to mean that it had been his feeling of insecurity that was responsible for his continuous failure?'

–'No, it's his dirty mind. Whether it is manipulation or sabotage, in fact, it is he who did all that to me. He couldn't do any harm to my success, but he could break my happy family any way.'

–'How?' Pihu wants to know everything about Aryan.

Aryan too reciprocates unhesitatingly. He tells her the whole story from the very beginning.

–'I met Maria, my ex-wife, at a common friend's party. That time I was shooting for a Kannada film in Bangalore. It was just a casual party. Then we met again after the success of my film 'Blind'. She was not only the daughter of one of the top builders of Mumbai, Mr. Rajan Raheja, but also a close friend of Riyanka. So we met for the second time at Riyanka's birthday party and hence things started changing. We were getting attracted to each other. In the meantime Maria suddenly asked her father to produce a film with me as hero and she the heroine. Contrary to all my objections, just to fulfill his daughter's wish, Mr. Raheja made a huge-budget film. During the shoot we came too close, and decided to get married after the film's release; and the industry witnessed a big gala wedding of Mr. Rajan Raheja's only pampered daughter.

The film didn't sell much in the market as expected. But she gave me the greatest gifts of my life within the next four years—Armaan and Ananya.

But soon after problems started cropping up and our conjugal relation started deteriorating every day.

During that period Sahryar and a few of his pets played a dirty game with my family being envious of my success.

Right since the beginning Maria had been too possessive about me; but that was okay. But after a couple of years or so, this leaning of her started turning out into a bad habit. She started becoming curious every now and then about each and every of my female co-actor. It was getting disturbing, rather embarrassing for me. And Sahryar took full advantage of this ever increasing rift between us.

Maria had a friends' group. They used to hang out together. All were rich women—irrespective of whether they were married or unmarried. Their only work was to have pleasure and gossiping on the money of their husbands or fathers. Then one day, Sahryar's country-sister Shabnam Qureshi took entry into that nonsense group. Shabnam was Mumbai film-industry's one of the most popular model coordinators as well as the owner of a talent-hunt company. Shabnam's reach was beyond Mumbai up to Delhi; even she had some minister's in her…. Anyway, within a short time Shabnam became a close friend of Maria and started brainwashing her gradually against me.'

Pihu inquires with a commonsense-note, 'Why didn't you make her understand when you knew it?'

Aryan says in reply, 'How could I know then? During that period I had been working in 2-3 films simultaneously. Monali Shah was my heroine in one of those. She was definitely different from the rest of the heroines. Besides acting she was updated in various trades—politics, sports, music etc. You could talk to her; that way, she was interesting too apart from being attractive. She wasn't a dud like others.

So, within a few days we became good friends. But I was not in the know that Monali was introduced to the director of the film by Shabnam planfully with Sahryar's instigation. Controversy began right from the promotional photo shoot session and busted on the day Monali gave an interview just before the release of the film. Where, before all the press and media-persons she gave the statement that we—meaning she and I—were attacked to each other in every way, mentally and physically. That statement of her of course did help a lot in giving a bumper opening of the film, but the doubt Maria had about me turned into a belief.

It had already been too late before I could grasp the whole thing. But these people just didn't stop there. To get me out of the film industry, ruin my social and family life, they started launching attacks one after another. All these things continued. Finally, somehow though I could restore my image and place in the industry, I could not save my family from breaking. The gap between us went on widening. Then one day Maria talked to her dad and left for his home with the children.

God gifted me two best prizes of my life; my children—Armaan and Ananya—were just snatched away from me by a single blow. Ananya still misses me all the time. Once a week she comes to meet me. It was such a strange chance that the year I bought my mother, brother and sister a new flat in Mumbai and brought them in, my own family left my home the same year. The public accepted Aryan Kapoor by and by, but Maria and Raheja family didn't accept me again.

Pihu takes her time to react. That is obvious for a normal person, brought in a family with natural Indian values far from the apparently glittering world of cinema.

She says, 'How strange is all this, isn't it?'

–'Yes, this industry is really strange in itself' Aryan says in admission.

A baffled Pihu asks, 'Sahryar Khan himself came from outside of Mumbai and obviously had to struggle a lot to make a place for himself in the film industry—especially when the industry is dominated by star families. What can't I understand, how does such a person, instead of helping a struggling person, want to destroy his career?'

Aryan replies instantly, 'It's owing to lack of unity.'

–'I didn't get you', Pihu says.

Aryan clears the thing. He says, 'You see Pihu, it's not that there is no competition among these star-families; that they don't conspire against one another. But whenever fingers are raised against any of them from others, they all get united and stand by the alleged. But we outsiders? We all are fragmented in our self made dreams. We think, when I had to make so much struggle to secure my place, why should the other get that so easily? And that's where jealousy and sense of insecurity come into play.'

Pihu remarks, 'Really it is sad and pathetic. Nepotism is a curse. Sometimes it puzzles me to think whether we are living in the 21st. century or in the time of kings and queens!'

Aryan shares his experience with his ardent, honest and patient listener– may be for the first and last time of his life. He says, 'Pihu, cinema is a thankless job to say the least; and life is all about "survival of the fittest". Anyway, let's leave it here. When the very person, who supposedly was to feel all this could not be convinced....after all words have their limitations.'

Pihu looks at the clock. It is far beyond midnight. Then she looks at Aryan, who obviously looks tipsy. She hastens to say, 'I think you should now go to sleep. At least for a while.'

–'Yes, feeling really sleepy. Held you too for so long...'

Pihu assures him with a smile that it's fine with her.

Before leaving, thankfully Aryan says, 'But to be true, it's been a long time since I talked with someone at length... pouring out my heart unfiltered, uncensored! Thank you very much for your time. Good Night.

Pihu leaves for her room, saying, 'Good night. See you.'

One night's tete-a-tete with Pihu brings forth an astonishing change in Aryan.

On the next morning of the 28th.of March he wakes up early and gets out for a jog behind the bungalow. He finds a beautiful brook streaming almost at the doorstep. Aryan gets stunned by the abundance of nature's beauty.

Aryan, a broken depressed fastidious man till yesterday night, suddenly feels rejuvenated.

He sees a paper boat floating on the book's stream crossing him. At a little distance Aryan notices a beautiful girl child donned in traditional attire making a paper boat. He walks down to her and waves. The pixy girl smiles back. Aryan takes a picture of her with his mobile camera and leaves with a contented smile in his leaps.

Jogging, he enters the bungalow's lawn. Pihu comes on to the balcony with a cup of coffee in her hand. She notices Aryan, feels pleased to see a refreshed lively Aryan on the glittering green grass of the lawn in the bright sunshine under a spotless blue sky.

Pihu waves at him showing her cup gesturing if Aryan wants to have coffee. He shows his flask in reply. Both smile at each other.

Aryan starts exercising. Pihu can't resist her coming down to the lawn.

To her utter surprise she sees a totally changed man in Aryan—a swaggering bright handsome person beaming with a new lease of life.

Pihu feels tempted to tease Aryan. She, with an alluring smile in her lips exclaims that he really then wakes up in the morning!

Aryan also doesn't fail to answer smartly that though every news about him isn't right, all are not wrong too!

She happily lets him know that one of his diehard fans, Chhutki, would really be happy to know that.

Aryan's free mind gets nostalgic. He talks about his mother who used to get angry if he got up late in the morning. Thus, it's his old practice to rise early in the morning. Sharing his view with his new compatible young friend, he says that to spend some time with oneself in the calmness of early morning, more so with so much of natural beauty around, is a medicine in itself—an impossibility in dangerously polluted Mumbai.

Pihu agrees, referring to Delhi's case where she practices.

However, she tells him that her father was looking for him and he might be waiting for Aryan at the breakfast table in the lawn.

Aryan tells her that surely he will be sharp there. He also thanks Pihu for listening to him last night so patiently.

Pihu reciprocates with a friendly smile and says that in no way that was a big deal. She leaves telling to see him at the breakfast table.

In midst of a family conversation in which Mr. Prabhakar is being coaxed by his family members along with their caretaker to have a glassful of bitter gourd-juice as per the advice of their family physician Dr. Malhotra, Aryan along with

Mishraji and Deepak join them at the breakfast table.

During a mixed conversation among the host and the guests regarding hospitality, wherein guests are all praise for their care with personal touch, though Prabhakar talks about his helplessness under stress owing to lockdown, Mishraji's phone rings.

He talks for a couple of minutes and informs all that a helicopter will land next morning to take them off to Mumbai. He does not miss to mention that the aviation department has given permission treating this as a special case.

In all probability, as Pihu thought, Aryan–who had, right since the declaration of lockdown and their resultant forced stay in Manali, been mostly perturbed–would now be feeling mostly relaxed for sure. But the human mind is strange; one never knows what drives it to think how!

Aryan and Pihu, by some chance, find themselves at the breakfast table with one another after the rest had left.

Pihu says to Aryan, 'So… now you must be feeling relaxed!'

–'Don't know exactly.'

–'Why? I mean, you're going back to your world!?'

With a shade of remorse in his voice Aryan says, 'Yes, that's true of course. But here, totally detached from that world for the last few days…far from the madding crowd…you know…I had a pure peace of mind I never knew before.'

Pihu says, 'That's good. This way—taking a break from work once in a while and just leave for some distant place. You will definitely feel better.'

Somewhat unsurely Aryan reflects, 'I don't know if I would have the same sort of feeling in a planned tour. And then, I'll have to have a psychotherapist like you with me to listen to me without being bored. Isn't it?"

Aryan ends with a laugh. Pihu smiles.

Aryan continues, 'In fact, my feeling at this moment is that I don't want any type of distraction. Presently I'm at peace with myself. I can't tell you exactly the reason. But it's just like that.

Here I feel really nice. On return, I'll miss this place. Maybe it will take some time to get myself adjusted. In fact I, or you may say men like we actors, don't know–rather say, haven't learnt–anything except acting. What else do we have in our life besides these film-set-camera-light etc.? Here every Friday our future changes. That day of the week gives us both— extreme discomfort or ultimate peace in turn. That is our very place. Anyway, leave my story. One thing I must admit in a way is that you people are too nice— Prabhakarji, your mom, you... Kishanlal, Chhutki... everyone. It has really been nice talking to you all. That way, it is by liking you people I started liking this place, thought of late. I think all places are more or less the same; it's the people that make the difference, to make it good or bad for the visitor.

Pihu admits his observation and then suddenly asks Aryan an uncanny question.

She says to Aryan, 'Well, tell me one thing. If one day suddenly you lose this stardom, popularity, everything that you've achieved, would you have the same passion as you have at the moment?'

Aryan takes a pause to get himself ready for a long answer.

He says, 'I can get what you want to know about. With the passage of time the tastes of viewers are changing. I'm too ageing. Competition is getting tougher everyday. Next generation, new actors–quite talented..well trained..well groomed, all are emerging thick and fast. But I tell you Pihu, these young people do the acting okay, perform well too; but they don't live life with the film, rather cinema, like us. Just have it that, we remain to be very a few of those actors who only eat film, drink film and sleep on it under its cover. No way; just to live or die for it. And the most important thing we have is our experience. I don't have any degree of any kind from a film school, but I know the work of every department—camera, light, direction. I've learnt everything that makes a film. Because I believe that acting is not just a performing art that starts with the director's shout: 'action', and ends with 'cut'.

You have got to live with it every moment, mentally- physically-emotionally till its end. And one more thing—I have fallen many times but got up every time; and thus only I've reached where I'm. So, now I'm no more afraid of a fall. It is not easy now to raze the house built on a foundation laid with such strong intent. And even if this building gets demolished, I will be able to rebuild the same again. But what may come, this Cinemawala will live the cinema till the end..

Pihu ends the conversation aptly quoting the first line of a song of a legendary Hindi movie of yesteryear: 'Jina yahan, marna yahan; iske siwa, Jana kahan'.

At last, after many a conjecture stuffed with thousand and one 'ifs' and 'buts', the much desired helicopter lands on Mr. Prabhakar's lawn the next morning.

While Kishanlal and Chhutki are carrying all their luggage onto the lawn and the others are busy this or that way, Aryan comes up to the balcony having seen Pihu with the cup of coffee in her hands.

Aryan agrees to Pihu's offer for a cup of coffee for the first time and the last time. They get involved in some casual talks, though somewhere deep within both are feeling a bit of the pang of separation.

In between the conversations Aryan says that he didn't expect Pihu in the early morning as he had seen her room's light on beyond late night.

Pihu informs that she had been working on a painting all through to get that finished before going to bed.

On asking whether she paints portraits, Pihu says that she doesn't until is impressed by someone's persona like, for instance, her father's.

They were just biding time together as long as possible before leaving, as they grew a sort of liking for each other, for different reasons though. Obviously, the conversation was casual.

But, maybe by chance, Aryan wants to know from Pihu how she felt about a film star looking from so close.

Pihu in a jestly tone asks, 'From a doctor's viewpoint or that of an artist's?'

Aryan replies that it would be better to know her view as an artist; as because, if her remarks as a doctor prescribes any changes for him to bring about in him, that wouldn't be possible for him to follow.

Pihu thinks for a moment, pauses to finish her coffee, puts it on the table and then says, 'To be true, I also, like the rest, used to think of you people as some show-plant—tender, delicate—that need extra care; to be watered, taken to sunlight in time…to get bloomed.

But now I think I was mistaken. In last few days I've come to realize that you too are like the rest of the normal people who always hide their reality behind a mask. And being a painter I at least know that an artist happens to be much more emotional than an average person. He or she has got to be emotional if he craves to create something. Maybe you have been hurt a thousand times, suffered a lot mentally, felt grieved deep into your heart during all this 25-30 years' journey. But that could not lessen your passion and obsession with film ever. It's so inspiring for others!

Actually…you know what? You are like the phoenix bird that rises up from its ashes. The actor in you would never die. He will always resurrect from his grave.

But I have a small piece of advice for you. It is not good for your mental health to let your emotions lose in acting only and then to suppress those outside it. That your personal emotions fall flat on someone's feelings, doesn't mean you should shut all the doors of your heart for all. Presently it is so that, someone can at best come near you but can't enter into your soul.

Aryanji, if there can be retakes in reel-life why can't that come into play in real life? And that life has given you so much! Now it's your turn to pay back; to allow your real life to have at least a retake to get things properly placed. Have I said anything wrong?'

Aryan just keeps on looking at Pihu….desperately groping for words to communicate his heart's sincere feeling to what she said at the last moment. But before he could say anything Deepak arrives at the spot hurriedly to take him downstairs, as everything was ready for their departure.

But Aryan couldn't help himself ; somewhat over passing Deepak's rush, he turns around to say his last words to Pihu—a person he found so understanding and caring. He says to her, 'Okay Pihu, see you then. Don't know when we shall meet again. But I must remember your advice. As of now, bye. Take care.'

Pihu also bids adieu.

Before stepping out towards the exit Aryan assures his lady of choice that he has decided to do a couple of films for serious and rational viewers, and hopes she must see those.

Pihu encouragingly replies that she will of course see his films and she also knows that he would do far better.

At last, the propeller starts roaring and the helicopter, the much-awaited desired rescuer, takes off.

When Mishraji and Deepak were waving back to Mr. and Mrs. Prabhakar's au-revoir signal, Chhutki saw Aryan waving at the balcony where her Pihu didi was also waving with a pensive look!

Fourteen days' quarantine is over after they reach Mumbai.

Aryan is playing a video game on play station at his room to bide time in the afternoon when Mishraji comes.

After a long time Aryan hears some real good news from his ever well wisher.

Mishraji very cheerfully informs him that the whole post-production processing of the film has just been completed that day. He and Bobby saw the film a few hours back. It has been made superbly. Mishraji tells Aryan cheerfully that this film as well as the mode and quality of his acting is quite different from all of his previous ventures. He remarks that Aryan has really done a great job.

Mishraji lets him know that Bobby will come in the evening to meet him. Further he says, quoting Bobby, that owing to shut-down of theatres for lockdown, OTT-viewership has grown too much, and someone has already offered him a hundred twenty core deal. He wishes Aryan all the success with the grace of God.

And all this—Mishraji's demeanor, his attitude— in turn overwhelms Aryan.

He can't help telling his mentor, 'Mishraji, whatever has still been achieved and to be had ahead, for all the happenings, you are the reason. It's all your brain child. But for all this, you give me the whole credit without demanding anything in return.'

Mishraji, shrugging off Aryan's appreciation, as an honest mentor should do, lovingly tells him to leave all this for the present. He takes leave of him somewhat in a hurry telling Aryan that the situation outside is not good. Before departing he hands him over a cylindrical case saying, 'It is a gift for you from Pihu. I forgot to give it to you.'

Taking the packing Aryan thanks him and tells him to take care.

Mishraji stops at the exit of the door, turns around, looks in his eyes and tells Aryan, 'She is really a nice girl.'

No sooner had Mishraji left, Aryan gets a Whatsapp message from Radhika, his heroine. She has asked him to watch the news.

Aryan instantly switches the television set on wherein he finds a debate is on about him.

To be exact, some of Aryan's co-actresses along with Radhika are taking part in a panel discussion defending him against the allegation put on him by Natasha.

Nonchalantly Aryan looks at the TV-screen....

ANCHOR: The famous actress Radhika has joined us. Radhikaji, what's your opinion on Natasha Khandelwal's allegations against Aryan Kapoor?

RADHIKA: Total nonsense! It's nothing but a cheap publicity stunt. I have acted with him in not less than three films. I know him well enough. You just ask any junior female artist in the industry about Aryan Kapoor who has acted with him. Far from being insolent or philanderer, he is very much protective about women to the contrary.

ANCHOR: You talked of junior female artists. Ayesha Bhatia has joined us in the meantime. Ayesha, you were Aryan's younger sister in the film 'Teri Bindiya'. How was your experience with him?

AYESHA BHATIA: First of all, I totally agree with Radhika ma'am. I was very nervous on the set. Aryan sir came and talked to me to make me feel at ease and comfortable with the situation. So much so, he always made sure that I get a separate car from the production to go home after the pack. Tell me about just one superstar who bothers so much for a junior artist.

And, as of Natasha— I know her too well as having been her flat-mate. She is a cry-baby to say the least. She wants everything in her life without labour and perseverance. And this drama of hers is nothing new.

Aryan switches the TV off; looks at the dead screen of the idiot box for a while. He finds himself in a dilemmatic state of mind— feeling resigned and relaxed at the same time.

Aryan takes a deep breath. He looks at the gift-pack sent by Pihu. He opens the case. Surprisingly, he finds a canvas-size painting. It's a colorful painting of a Phoenix Bird with Aryan's face on.

Aryan smiles and gently caresses the painting. He goes to another room, opens a cabinet to take out a frame. He carefully fixes the painting on it. Then he hangs the painting on the wall of his bedroom that he faces while lying on his bed.

He looks at it again for a while; now from a distance. Aryan takes out his mobile phone and takes a selfie with the painting behind him.

Finally, he lights a cigarette, lies down on the bed in his back and stares at Pihu's painting.

One doesn't know exactly, though may guess on what he is reflecting upon presently. But one thing seems certain from his body language that at this very moment he feels relieved. May be thinking of Pihu's 'small advice' of starting a second innings to give himself a chance of rearranging his personal deranged life in some way or the other…who knows?

However, at heart Aryan thanks Pihu, maybe not for the last time.

www.ingramcontent.com/pod-product-compliance
Lightning Source LLC
LaVergne TN
LVHW041615070526
838199LV00052B/3157